CLASH IN THE UNDERWATER WORLD

AN UNOFFICIAL OVERWORLD HEROES ADVENTURE, BOOK FOUR

DANICA DAVIDSON

Sky Pony Press
New York

Sky Pony Press books may be purchased in bulk at special discounts for sales
promotion, corporate gifts, fund-raising, or educational purposes. Special
editions can also be created to specifications. For details, contact the Special
Sales Department, Sky Pony Press, 307 West 36th Street, 11th Floor,
New York, NY 10018 or info@skyhorsepublishing.com.

Sky Pony® is a registered trademark of Skyhorse Publishing, Inc.®,
a Delaware corporation.

Minecraft® is a registered trademark of Notch Development AB.
The Minecraft game is copyright © Mojang AB.

Visit our website at www.skyponypress.com.

10 9 8 7 6 5 4 3 2 1

The Library of Congress has cataloged this book as follows:

Names: Davidson, Danica, author.
Title: Clash in the underwater world / Danica Davidson.
Description: New York : Skyhorse Publishing, [2018]
Identifiers: LCCN 2018001522 (print) | LCCN 2018008921 (ebook) | ISBN
    9781510733503 (eb) | ISBN 9781510733480 (pb) | ISBN 9781510733503 (ebook)
Classification: LCC PZ7.D28263 (ebook) | LCC PZ7.D28263 Cl 2018 (print) | DDC
    [Fic]--dc23

Cover design by Brian Peterson
Cover photo by Lordwhitebear

Ebook ISBN: 978-1-5107-3350-3

Printed in Canada

CLASH IN THE UNDERWATER WORLD

CHAPTER 1

W E WERE IN THE MIDDLE OF THE OCEAN, AND we'd lost all sight of land. If anything went wrong, we'd be on our own.

In our little boat were Dad, my cousin Alex, my Earth friends, Maison, Destiny, and Yancy, and Yancy's newly tamed parrot, Blue. And me. But even though I was part of the Overworld Heroes task force, I felt small compared to this huge ocean with all its incredible creatures swimming just below the surface. I had had no idea how dangerous this mission would be until now—when it was too late.

Yancy wasn't helping any. In fact, he was really freaking me out.

"Hey, look at this one, Stevie," Yancy said cheerfully, showing me another picture. He'd pulled some book about ocean life on Earth out of that backpack he was always carting around. Now he was flipping through pages, showing me creatures that looked like they'd come straight from my nightmares.

I stared at the image of a hideous fish with a mouth full of row after row of fangs. On its head was a prong with a small, glowing light on the end of it, like a tiny sea lantern. If anything like that fish was waiting in the ocean below us, I'd rather just stay on the boat.

"This is an anglerfish," Yancy said. Blue, who was perched on Yancy's shoulder, whistled. "They live in the deep ocean and can grow up to three feet. They even *glow* because of bacteria down there. It's so dark in the deep ocean that you wouldn't be able to see a thing unless you bring your own light or see fish glowing. Some of the fish use their glow to lure in their prey. And the pressure is so bad down there that if you don't go in a submarine, the weight of the water will crush you."

I didn't know what being crushed by water pressure felt like, but my stomach was squeezing pretty badly on its own. And my mouth was getting dry just looking at that anglerfish.

"Yancy, stop it," Destiny sighed. "You know the ocean in *Minecraft* isn't the same as the ocean on Earth. There aren't any anglerfish here, and I don't think it gets that dark, either."

"Hey, there could be anglerfish. And who knows how dark it gets?" Yancy said. "On Earth, we're still discovering new sea life because the ocean is so big. And you know that some of the creatures we have on Earth are also in *Minecraft*. Like Blue." He gestured to his new parrot pet. Earlier Yancy had said that being in a boat with a parrot made him look even more like a pirate. But when no one had paid much attention to that, he'd pulled out his book instead. And this agony began.

"See, look at this," Yancy said, turning another page. "A pufferfish! We have those in both places!"

Next to the anglerfish, the pufferfish looked pretty okay to me. "My dad has hunted pufferfish to make the Potion of Water Breathing," I said, looking at Dad. I wanted him to tell me that pufferfish weren't too bad. And that even though lots of the Overworld ocean hadn't been explored yet, there was no way we'd run into any anglerfish.

Unfortunately, Dad was busy looking at the map. Normally, we'd have had to go to a special cartographer in the village to get an ocean map. But we had our own special map thanks to Steve Alexander, my ancestor, who had left us the clues we needed to find Ender crystal shards that could be used to make a special weapon to defeat the Ender Dragon. Each time we completed another mission, the crystal shard we found helped us read more of Steve Alexander's magical book, which showed us where we had to go next.

Clearly, Dad wasn't going to be any help. Yancy went on, "Some people eat pufferfish on Earth, which is really dangerous if you don't do it right. They're toxic. If you eat the bad part, you'll be poisoned."

I gulped. "Well, we don't like to eat pufferfish in the Overworld," I said. "Because if you do, it makes you nauseated."

"Yancy, put the book away," Maison said, her arm hanging off the side of the boat so her fingers could trail through the waves. She looked as annoyed as Destiny was with how Yancy was acting. Alex was the only one who was staring at the book with gleeful fascination. The creepier the fish, the more interested she looked.

"Not till we get to the sharks," Yancy said, flipping the pages quickly. "Here you go, Stevie. Take a look at the great white shark."

I saw an enormous mouth, even bigger than the anglerfish's, with even larger teeth. The anglerfish had lots of tiny, jutting fangs, but the great white shark had a forest of triangular teeth with jagged edges.

"The great white shark can grow up to twenty-one feet long," Yancy read.

Twenty-one feet! I never thought an anglerfish could seem safe by comparison!

"Dad," I said in a slow voice, turning to him. What I wanted to say was: *Dad, please tell me Yancy is wrong and we don't have these fish here!*

"Not now, Stevie," Dad said with a frown. He was still studying the map in Steve Alexander's book. "We should be near the ocean monument holding the next crystal shard."

"Yancy, can you ride one of those?" Alex asked, pointing to the great white shark. I could tell she was already in love with the shark. "I bet they swim fast."

"If you try to ride it, it will probably eat you," Destiny said matter-of-factly.

Yancy looked up from his book in disgust. "Sharks don't go around eating people!" he said. "That's just a myth, and people believe it because they see it in movies. Sharks have more to fear from people than we do from them."

"Then what about shark attacks?" Destiny countered.

"They usually take a bite and then stop," Yancy said, as if this made everything okay. "They bite to try to figure out what something is, because they don't have hands like us. And anyway, shark attacks are incredibly rare. I'm sick of sharks getting a bad rap."

"Says the one trying to scare Stevie by showing him shark pictures," Maison muttered under her breath.

Yancy shut the book and tossed it dramatically on the floor of the boat. "I'm just trying to get us prepared for this mission. I've never been in the Overworld ocean before."

To tell the truth, I hadn't either. And that thought kept growing and growing in my head, like a pufferfish puffing itself up.

"Hey, if you're in shark territory, you're in *their*

space," Yancy went on. For some reason, he was really worked up about this. "They're just trying to eat to stay alive, and if people are being careless and in the shark's hunting grounds, they might get bitten. But don't blame the shark. It's not like in *Minecraft*, where you have hostile mobs that attack you for no clear reason."

Even though I was still nervous, I thought Yancy had an interesting point. If sharks had to eat, they had to eat, even if I thought they were scary looking. And if something unfamiliar was in the water, they had to figure out what it was, right? On the other hand, if we ran into any hostile mobs underwater—"mobs" was another word we used for "monster"—then they'd attack us just because they can, not because they need to in order to survive.

"Do you know you can pay to go under the water in a cage and have the great white sharks come right up to you?" Yancy asked. "I want to do that someday."

"Cool!" Alex cheered. "How many emeralds does it cost?"

"Why would anyone pay money for that?" Destiny asked at the same time, making a face.

"The cage keeps you safe, and there's a boat right there next to it," Yancy explained.

"I heard that sharks circle their prey," Destiny said. "What if they start circling your boat?"

"I know where you're going with this, but it's not going to happen," Yancy said. "As long as you're in a boat, nothing is going to hurt you."

That's when something leaped out of the waters and landed, with a screech, in our boat.

CHAPTER 2

GRABBED MY DIAMOND SWORD, STUNNED. FOR THE briefest second, I thought it might be an anglerfish or a pufferfish or even a great white shark. But it was a guardian, one of the fish known in the Overworld. And it was hostile.

The fish was flopping around, able to breathe in water or out of it. It was green and had rows of orange spikes all over its body, like a set of fangs outside of its mouth. The fish *kerplunk*ed right into Yancy's lap, making him yelp and jump back.

Even though I had my sword, I froze. The guardian had a single eye in its broad forehead, and it was staring right at me. I knew that was a bad sign. When a guardian stared at you, it meant you were its prey.

With a roar, Dad jumped to his feet and struck the

guardian with his sword, all while I sat frozen under the fish's creepy gaze. I felt like I was hypnotized.

"Whoa, Uncle Steve!" Alex said to Dad, impressed. The fish disappeared and dropped some prismarine crystal shards. "I didn't know they could jump into boats like that!"

I caught Yancy's eye. He had backed himself into the far end of the boat, panting and sweaty. For the first time, I realized he was scared, himself. Maybe he had been showing me all that Earth ocean stuff to try to share his fear, or to act tough, or something.

"You kids need to stop jabbering about Earth fish and pay attention," Dad said sternly. I noticed then that he was hurt and trying not to show it. His sword hand was trembling a little, and he put his other hand on top of it to steady it. "Of course they can jump into boats. They can also electrocute you while you're in your boat and they're still in the water."

"But that's why we've got this armor," Alex said. For good measure, she pounded her fist against the iron armor she had on.

When Dad had learned our next crystal shard mission would take us to an ocean monument, he had said we needed to get armor made—no ifs, ands, or buts. I'd always dreamed of having diamond armor some-day, but Dad had said we didn't have time to mine diamonds. With the village blacksmith's help, we'd quickly made ourselves sets of iron armor. It turned out the armor for the Earth kids was a little trickier to make because they had different body proportions.

"The armor helps," Dad said. "However, it doesn't protect you entirely. If you touch the guardians when their spikes are extended, you will get hurt. I have some milk for us to drink so that we can heal, but we don't have a lot of it."

That was why Dad was hurt. I knew guardians could extend and pull in their spikes, but the guardian in our boat had had its spikes out the whole time.

Dad narrowed his eyes at us. "And what did I say about guardians?"

We all looked down. That's just the posture you find yourself in when you're getting lectured. There's no helping it.

"When they're getting ready to shoot you with their lasers, they start shooting out sizzling purple rays," I mumbled. "You only have a few seconds to fight or get out of the way. Then the rays turn yellow and zap you. You can hide behind columns to avoid being zapped, or you can swim right at them, or you can get out of their range. Otherwise . . ."

"Otherwise, we're not going to have enough milk for you all," Dad said. "We had to set out before the Ender Dragon's minions, so there wasn't time to collect a lot of supplies. We only have a few bottles of the Potion of Water Breathing and the Potion of Night Vision, and we have to use those sparingly. You won't be able to see underwater well without the Potion of Night Vision, and you definitely won't be able to stay underwater long without the Potion of Water Breathing. I used everything I had in my supply shed to even get this much."

Dad used to have the best supply shed around, until a Wither attack destroyed it. Now, when it came to supplies, he just had odds and ends that somehow hadn't been ruined. It took bottled water, one Nether wart, and one pufferfish to make the Potion of Water Breathing. It took bottled water, one Nether wart, and one golden carrot to make a Potion of Night Vision. I knew Dad had snagged a few extra pieces of Nether wart to bring along, just in case, but there weren't any more golden carrots or pufferfish around.

"I still think it would be safer if I went to the ocean monument alone," Dad said, looking at us.

"No, Uncle Steve!" Alex whined. "We want to go too! We're the Overworld Heroes!"

That was a name Alex's mom, Aunt Alexandra, had given Alex, Maison, Yancy, Destiny, and me. Dad still didn't seem to care much for us being a task force and wouldn't let us go alone on these missions. But the Ender Dragon was growing stronger, so we didn't have time to bicker. Longer nights were a symbol of the Ender Dragon's power back in the days of Steve Alexander, and we were seeing those longer nights happening again. She had also been speaking to me in my head, though lately she'd been suspiciously quiet. When she'd been howling her evil words at me, I'd wished she'd go away. Now I was worried about what her silence meant. She must be up to something.

"Besides the guardians, we might also run into elder guardians," Dad said, choosing not to respond to Alex's whining. She was lucky she wasn't his kid. If I'd been the one whining, I sure would have heard about it! "These fish are much bigger and they will hit you with Mining Fatigue if you get close to them."

"We get Mining Fatigue in *Minecraft* too," Maison said. "It will make it harder to mine, but we're not here for that. We just need to find the crystal and get out."

"That's exactly right," Dad said. "We are not tarrying there." He put Steve Alexander's book in front of us so we could all read his words again. I tried to imagine Steve Alexander writing this thousands of years ago with his quill pen, warning his descendants.

There is much yet to be discovered in the depths of the ocean, he'd written. *The guardians' lasers will burn you, so bring armor. To your left and to your right, there will be elder guardians. Avoid them as best you can. Find the glow, and find your treasure.*

"Every ocean monument has three elder guardians," Dad informed us. "One in each wing and one in the top. Steve Alexander is telling us to stay away from them, so at least that seems to be a clue that the crystal shard is not in any of those rooms. Let's be grateful for that."

Alex looked very disappointed.

Maison said, "I bet it's still difficult, though. If it were too easy, the Ender Dragon's minions might find the shard."

Yes. The Endermen were the main minions of the Ender Dragon, though lately she'd gotten other hostile mobs to fight us, like zombies and armed skeletons. I hoped the fish weren't on her side as well.

"What do you think he means by 'find the glow, and find your treasure'?" Maison asked. "Is it just because the crystal shard will glow?"

"I think it has to do with the sea lanterns you find in ocean monuments, because they also glow," Alex said. "I think we should check around all of those first. I want to collect some to decorate my bedroom, anyway."

"No," Dad said firmly. "We are not bringing back any souvenirs. We are bringing back the Ender crystal. And. That. Is. It."

He was treating us all like babies, I thought. Dad had been to ocean monuments before to collect the gold you could find there, but he'd told me he didn't care for them and preferred to stay on land. Because of that, I'd never been out to the open ocean like this. The only things I knew about ocean monuments were from books I'd taken out of the village library and from stories Dad had told me about his own adventures.

"Any other questions?" Dad asked. The way he was looking at us made us want to say no. He was especially glaring at Yancy, and I knew Yancy felt it. Blue the parrot was the only one oblivious to the intensity, and he was happily chirping away.

"Wait, I think I see it!" Maison exclaimed, pointing a little farther into the distance. "Something is glowing below the water!"

CHAPTER 3

FIRST I SAW THE VAGUE GLOWING, AND AS DAD steered the boat closer, the form of the ocean monument became visible.

"It's beautiful," Destiny said, as if she couldn't believe it.

"It's dangerous," Yancy corrected darkly, frowning down at it.

A castle was sprawled on the ocean floor, made of aqua-colored prismarine blocks and decked with the glowing, box-shaped sea lanterns that had first alerted Maison to its location. It was probably as big as the enormous jungle temple we'd found the last crystal shard in, with rooms and rooms and rooms. The ocean monument stood flanked with columns, and I could just barely see some of the sea life floating in and around it.

"All right, kids," Dad said, turning to us. "You each have two Potions of Night Vision and two Potions of Water Breathing. And that's all we have, understood?"

We nodded.

"I can't wait to go pop some guardians with my arrows!" Alex said, one of the potions already halfway to her mouth. Dad put his hand out and stopped her.

"Your arrows won't work as well underwater," he said. "You will be at a disadvantage, Alex. We all will, because we can't move as fast underwater. We didn't have time to make any Potions of Swiftness."

"There are enchantments to help you underwater too," Yancy said, trying to be useful. "I like to use them when I play the game *Minecraft*."

Uh-oh. I looked at Dad. Yancy had just done two bad things: he'd questioned Dad's knowledge, and he'd referred to our world as a *game*. Sometimes I thought Yancy never learned.

"I don't do enchantments," Dad said stiffly, eyeing Yancy.

"I was just saying you could try something new—" Yancy began.

"Who on this boat has been to an ocean monument before?" Dad cut in. "And not just in a *game*?" He said the word "game" with real disgust.

Everyone got quiet, even Alex.

"I thought so," Dad said. "Drink your potions, and let's dive in. The Potion of Water Breathing will let us talk to one another in the water. When it starts to get hard to talk, that's when you know the potion is almost worn out. Then we'll take another potion. When it starts getting harder to see, then it's time for another Potion of Night Vision. If we take them at the same time, they'll both stop working at about the same time. Any questions?"

What if we don't have enough potion? I thought. I bit my tongue.

Dad looked at Yancy. Yancy shook his head, looking uncomfortable under Dad's glare. Behind them, Alex was already chugging both her potions.

"I'm ready, Uncle Steve!" she called out and dove below the surface with a splash. I lifted the two pinkish potions to my mouth, drinking one and then the other. I tried to catch Yancy's eyes with mine, but he wouldn't look at me. Dad, Maison, and Destiny all quickly swigged their potions, and Dad jumped in after Alex. Maison was next, followed by Destiny a moment later. Destiny hesitated for the briefest moment before she dove.

Then it was just Yancy and me in the boat. And Blue, except Blue didn't count.

"Ready, Yancy?" I asked.

Yancy was drinking his potions as if they were medicine that didn't taste good. He crawled over to the edge of the boat with me and we both looked down. Neither one of us jumped.

"You first," Yancy said.

"No," I said. "You first."

"Why? Are you scared, Stevie?" Yancy asked.

I looked at Yancy. At first I had felt kind of bad for him, but now I was getting annoyed. "I wasn't the one who yelped when a guardian jumped into the boat," I reminded him.

"Hey, it jumped *on* me," Yancy said. "And I saw your eyes get pretty big too."

We both looked back down at the water.

"Have you ever been in the ocean on Earth?" I asked.

"Oh, sure, yeah," Yancy said. "But, like, at the beach. I've never been to the deep ocean."

"How come?" This made me curious. "You sure seem into the ocean."

Yancy made a face as if he were still tasting bad medicine. "Well, there's a difference between appreciating the majesty of sea life in the safety of your own home . . . and, like I said, going out into sea life's territory."

So he *was* scared.

"Okay, I know how we'll decide this," Yancy said after a moment. "Rock, paper, scissors."

"What?" I said, confused.

"It's a game we play on Earth," Yancy said. "And whoever loses has to jump in first."

"Okay," I said slowly, wondering if there was a catch to this. "How do you play?"

"First, we both put our hands behind our backs. Then, on the count of three, we pull them out. We can make a rock hand, which looks like this, a paper hand, which looks like this, or a scissors hand, which looks like this." He demonstrated. "Rock beats scissors, scissors cuts paper, paper wraps up rock. Got it?"

Before I could answer, he put his hand behind his back. "One-two-three," he counted quickly, like it was all one word. He whipped his hand back out in front of mine, his hand flat. "Oh, I win!" he said. "Paper wraps around rock!"

Now I was just plain mad. "That's cheating, Yancy!" I said. "You know I can't move my hand like that!" I looked down at my own hand, frustrated. All I could do was the "rock" hand. And how could something as flimsy as paper beat rock, anyway? It didn't make any sense.

"If you don't like the results, we can do best two out of three," Yancy offered with an insincere smile.

I was about to tell Yancy what I thought of him and his game, but then another guardian leaped into the boat, landing between us. As it looked at me, it began to sizzle purple, getting ready to strike with its laser.

CHAPTER 4

"JUMP!" I CRIED. WITHOUT ANOTHER ARGUMENT, Yancy and I both dove overboard while Blue flew, squawking, into the air. I knew Blue would be fine on his own, because guardians wouldn't bother a bird.

Sinking beneath the water was as much like entering a whole new world as going through a portal into a completely different realm. On the surface, the water had seemed smooth and calm, but underneath it was teeming with life and action. Everything turned blue and I could see bubbles rising up from my mouth and going to the surface. Below me was a swarm of puffthe erfish beside orange and white clownfish, and ahead were a number of squid. As the squid moved, I could see their giant mouths tucked right up into them. I knew squid didn't attack people, but I was still thinking about being eaten by sea life.

"There you are," Alex scolded when she saw us. Her voice sounded funny, sort of like someone talking while gargling. "What took so long?"

"It doesn't matter," I said. I heard myself and realized I had the same gargling voice. That must be how people talked underwater when they'd taken the Potion of Water Breathing. "We're here."

"I was about to go up and get you," Dad said, floating a few feet away. He was looking back and forth between Yancy and me. "You can't take your time like that. Come on, let's go."

I had a feeling he wanted to lecture us some more but would wait until we were breathing air again to do it. Oh boy, I had something to look forward to.

"There's the entrance to the ocean monument," Dad said, gesturing with his diamond sword. "Kids, follow me. And watch out for guardians. The other fish won't bother you."

We all began swimming. Dad, Alex, and I swam like we were walking, only we were underwater. Maison, Destiny, and Yancy all swam differently. They looked more like they were lying down and they were pulling themselves forward with big sweeps of their arms while their feet kicked back behind them. Their hair was drifting all around their faces, moving in the currents. I thought it was a pretty weird way to swim, but that was Earth people for you.

None of us was very fast. Alex was looking less

excited as she realized how slowly we were making our way toward the monument. That said something, because Alex was always excited for a new adventure.

So far we hadn't run into any more guardians, but I could definitely see a bunch of them hanging out around the monument entrance, and I knew they weren't going to just let us slide right in. Thankfully, though, at the moment they were distracted. A giant squid was swimming by overhead, and the guardians were taking turns zapping it with their lasers. The squid disappeared and dropped an ink sac.

The guardians started shooting at another squid that had come their way. They were so cruel! This squid turned and began heading in the other direction, out of the guardians' range.

"Why do guardians hate squid so much?" Destiny wondered. "When I play *Minecraft*, they're always attacking squid."

"One of the mysteries of the Overworld, I guess," Alex said.

Mystery was right. When Yancy had said that Earth's seas were mostly unexplored, it made me realize how much we didn't know about our own Overworld oceans.

"Do you think the crystal shard is hidden with the gold?" Maison asked. "Every ocean monument has eight blocks of gold tucked away behind dark prismarine."

"We'll check there, though that might be too obvious," Dad said. He was gripping Steve Alexander's book. On Earth, books got ruined if you took them in water, but our Overworld books were a lot stronger.

Find the glow, and find your treasure. I heard Steve Alexander's words in my mind. He liked to talk in riddles, so what did that mean? I didn't think he meant the gold—that would be too obvious, because everyone would want to look for the gold in the monument. It was the same thing with the sea lanterns, because those were also things people would seek out.

So where would a hero genius like Steve Alexander hide a crystal shard? Would we have to mine the whole area to find it under the floor or in the walls? But what about the Mining Fatigue the elder guardians created? Would we run out of potions and have to go back to land and make more? What if the Ender Dragon's minions saw us leave the area and decided to check out the ocean monument for themselves? But Endermen couldn't stand water, so I knew they wouldn't come down here. Maybe that was why Steve Alexander chose to hide the crystal shard here: to keep the Endermen away.

As slowly as we were going, we were gradually getting closer to the columned entrance of the ocean monument. It was several stories high, much bigger than any of the houses Dad had ever made.

"It's like the lost city of Atlantis," Maison said in wonder.

I didn't know what Atlantis meant, but the ocean monument did look like a lost, forgotten part of some past age, buried into the ocean where only the bravest people would dare to go. Judging from Yancy's book, the Earth ocean was beautiful and fascinating, even if it was scary sometimes. So was the Overworld ocean. As we approached this monument, I had mixed feelings of awe and fear.

That scared feeling grew as the guardians realized there were much more interesting creatures in the water than squids. One by one, they turned their eyes on us.

CHAPTER 5

THE NEXT THING I KNEW WE WERE SURROUNDED, the guardians sizzling purple and getting ready to attack.

"Get behind the columns!" Dad yelled.

We rushed for the shelter of the columns, only to find that they were still too far away and we were too slow. I felt a jolt of electricity hit me from behind. Even with my iron armor on, the shock went through every inch of me. The blue water was now full of yellow and purple beams.

I was still trying to get my bearings when I felt myself get shocked again. There was no way I could make it to the columns if I kept getting attacked like this!

And it was hard to keep track of the others. I saw Maison barely swerve out of the way of a yellow blast.

Then she spun back around and hit the fish. Alex struck one guardian with her arrows, but the fish kept coming at her and she had to scurry away. It wasn't good enough. The guardian blasted Alex and I saw her whole body stiffen as she got hurt.

Yancy, who still had his backpack with him, swung it in front of his body like some sort of shield. When a yellow laser shot at him, I saw the backpack take the brunt of it, though Yancy was still shocked stiff for a second.

There was no way we could get through all this! Even now I could see more guardians swimming over, their fins swishing madly.

"Get behind the columns!" Dad hollered again. I lost sight of him somewhere in the blur of fins, single eyes, and blasting lasers.

I'm trying! I thought. I felt sore all over from those lasers.

A guardian got right in front of me and began to sizzle purple. I let out a startled cry, bubbles rushing from my mouth. My first instinct was to dart away, but I knew I didn't have time. Then I remembered what Dad had said: swimming at them made them pull back.

So, despite my instincts, I pushed myself toward the guardian. Just like that, the purple lights went away and it became docile. Normally I would never attack a docile mob, because I only believed in self-defense.

However, this *was* self-defense. If I didn't take it out now while I had the chance, it would get me as soon as I swam away.

When the guardian pulled back, it also let its spikes drop. I struck with my sword, noticing how the water slowed my swing. My diamond sword still hit the guardian and did damage. I hit it two more times, as fast as I could, and the guardian was gone.

Another one was coming at me, sparking up its purple laser. I pushed myself toward it and watched as it pulled back and drew in its spikes. I hit it with my sword several times and made it vanish. I was starting to get the hang of this!

But another one had slipped up from behind me. I didn't even see it or know it was there; I just felt another horrible shock shoot through me. I nearly dropped my sword.

I was almost to the columns, but I had to spin around to take care of this guardian. Before I finished turning all the way, I felt another shock.

"Argh!" I exclaimed. Everyone was so consumed in fighting the fish that no one could help anybody else. It was terrible, because normally we all fought as a team.

I floated there a moment, trying to regain my strength, while the guardian that had already hit me twice was getting ready for a third attack. They had to rest a few seconds between each laser blast, though unfortunately those few seconds didn't feel like enough time to recover after being hit. I looked straight into the guardian's single eye, which wouldn't leave my face for a second. Give me a great white shark or an anglerfish or a toxic pufferfish any day, I decided—anything but these cruel, unstopping guardians!

Hollering, Dad hurled himself through the water and struck the guardian. I watched in shock. The guardian's spikes were still out, so I knew Dad had gotten hurt attacking it, but he made the fish disappear. And it was a good thing, too, because it had almost beaten me.

"Dad!" I called out, scared. I could tell from the shaky way he held himself he must have been blasted a few times too. We were all in bad shape.

"Don't worry about me, Stevie!" Dad called back. "Get behind the columns!"

As much as I wanted to help, I knew the best thing to do right then was listen. I turned back toward the entrance of the ocean monument, pushing myself as fast as I could. If only we had had some Potion of Swiftness to help us move!

I stretched my arm in front of me as though I could reach out and touch a column. Closer, closer! There! My hand touched against the cool, turquoise side of a prismarine column, and I felt its strength and weight.

A guardian was coming at me, going purple. Just as it turned yellow, I pulled myself behind the column.

The yellow blast hit the column and not me, and I watched as sun-colored sizzles rushed to either side of the column, barely missing my body.

The next second Maison was there too, pulling herself behind the protective shield of the column.

"Are you hurt?" I asked her.

"This is worse than I thought," she admitted while trying to catch her breath. "I got hit a few times."

"Me too," I said. "Where are the others?"

A hand grabbed the edge of the column and Destiny pulled herself around. She also looked pretty shaken up.

"Where are Yancy, Alex, and Dad?" I asked.

They both looked at me with wide, I-have-no-idea eyes.

I peeked around the column. Yancy was trying to make his way over using his backpack for the little protection it gave him. Alex and Dad were in the thick of things, taking out one guardian after another. Dad was doing a better job with his sword than Alex was with her bow and arrows. Even as they took fish out, they were getting hit repeatedly. Especially Dad. How much more could he take?

"We've got to help them!" Destiny said.

I started to swim toward them with Maison and Destiny following. It felt bad going back out, but what else could we do? We needed to help the others get to the entrance with us.

"Yancy!" I shouted as we swam near him. He looked at me with frantic eyes. "We have to help Alex and my dad!" I went on.

Yancy looked over his shoulder, terrified. "You mean go back there?" he bleated.

"We don't have a choice!" I said.

Yancy heaved an enormous sigh and then slowly turned. Just as he did, a guardian came darting out of the depths, purpling. Before I could open my mouth to warn him, the guardian struck Yancy in a fire of yellow light.

"Owww!" Yancy cried. He hadn't been able to put his backpack at the right angle in time, and so he took on the full force of the blast. These guardians were unlike anything we'd ever faced before.

Dad saw us coming his way. "No, kids!" he shouted. "Get back behind the columns! Alex, go with them!"

That was all Yancy needed to hear. He took off again in the direction of the entrance.

"No, Uncle Steve!" Alex protested, only to be hit by a blast a moment later.

"Your arrows don't work well enough!" Dad shouted. "Go!"

Alex began scrambling our way, still shooting her arrows. When she reached Maison, Destiny, and me, we started heading back together. Yancy had already hidden himself on the other side of a column, barely dodging a yellow blast that hit the column instead of him.

As I swam, I looked back at Dad. He was battling the guardians and making them disappear so they couldn't just follow us into the monument. It needed to be done, but how many guardians might be inside the monument already?

"Hurry, Dad!" I called.

I shouldn't have said anything. Dad looked back at the sound of my voice and that distracted him long enough for another fish to get him. Dad stiffened and then his whole body sagged. He wasn't moving.

"No!" My voice was a wail now. Despite everything Dad had said, I started swimming back to him. Maybe I could grab him and pull him behind the column. We'd get some milk in him and then he'd be okay. As it was, I knew he was taking on all these blasts so he could better protect us!

"Stevie, wait!" Maison called.

The others all began shouting behind me. Their words were gargled, and their voices were echoing on top of one another, so I couldn't make out their words. It wasn't until the last moment I realized they were trying to warn me about a guardian rushing my way.

I turned my head and saw it. That single eye, enormous and close. Those spikes pointing out like fangs. And its purple light began to spark, readying for an attack.

I tried to dart away and toward it at the same time, my instincts pushing me one way and my mind another. As a result, I stumbled and knocked myself into the fish. My first thought was that if the laser didn't get me, running into the guardian would stick me full of spikes.

But I didn't feel any spikes. I didn't feel any laser, either. No, I felt something much worse. The guardian opened its mouth, and the next thing I knew I was inside it.

CHAPTER 6

I HAD BEEN EATEN ALIVE!

It was like being in a tiny red chamber. I barely fit, and I could see little gray and red blocks along the walls of the guardian's stomach, or whatever this place was.

Sharks on Earth might not go around eating people, but guardians in the Overworld did! What was I going to do? Could I get out of here? I tried to pull myself out through the guardian's mouth, but I was stuck. I knew I was just imagining it in my panic, yet I felt like the space was getting smaller and smaller, sucking me in. Let me out of here!

The guardian jolted, and I jolted with it. What had happened? There was another jolt, and then another. In an instant, I was back out in the blue ocean and the guardian was gone.

Alex stood a few feet away, her bow and arrows out. Her arrows still worked well enough underwater for her to finish off that guardian and release me.

"Alex!" I cried. I couldn't even say, *Thank you!* Or, *You saved me!* I was too shaken and relieved to even think straight.

"Just in a day's work," Alex said proudly.

Wait, what about Dad? I turned and saw Dad was still sagging helplessly in the water with his head down. Maison and Destiny had each grabbed one of his arms and were pulling him forward. They must have taken out the other guardians in the area, because I didn't see any.

"Stevie, you're all right," Dad breathed. His pain made him sound weak. "I couldn't get to you in time."

"It's all right, Dad," I said, swimming slowly over to him. "I'm okay." Right then I was more worried about him than me. Being sucked into the guardian had scared me, but I hadn't gotten hurt from it.

"Where's Yancy?" Destiny asked, looking around for him.

Yancy sheepishly peeked out from behind a column. "I'm here," he called in a low voice.

I was pretty sure I knew what had happened during the time I'd been swallowed: Alex had saved me, Maison and Destiny had gone to Dad's aid and taken out the other guardians, and Yancy had stayed hidden behind a column. That darn Yancy.

"Do you see any more guardians?" Maison asked.

"Not here," Alex said, looking around. "Let's get inside and have some milk before new ones find us."

Because more would find us, and we all knew it.

CHAPTER 7

SLOWLY, CAREFULLY, WE SWAM INTO THE ENORmous opening of the ocean monument. Maison and Destiny were still holding Dad, keeping him braced. We all looked up and around, amazed by the tall ceilings that towered over us.

"All ocean monuments have different sets of rooms, though they always have two wings," Dad was saying in his frail voice. Hurt or not, he wanted to keep us on top of things. "There's a room to the right. Go."

We swam into it. The room was small and empty, lined everywhere with turquoise stones. As soon as we were in there, Dad reached into his toolkit and pulled out a yellow, square-shaped sponge.

And what a difference that made! The sponge immediately began sucking up the water all around us. Outside this room everything was still blue ocean, and water lapped around our heels. But from our ankles up, the room was full of sweet, fresh air. Although the Potion of Water Breathing let us breathe under the water, it felt more natural to be in a space with actual air. I sucked the air deep into my lungs, savoring it.

"That's amazing," Yancy said. "Water doesn't work like that on Earth, so this is breaking all the rules of science. And, hey, Stevie, what was it like being inside the guardian? When you play *Minecraft*, you can accidentally slip inside them. I know, since—"

Yancy stopped talking. That's because Dad was giving him a not-another-word-out-of-you look.

"Yes, *game* knowledge from the one who hid," Dad said sarcastically. And Dad wasn't usually a sarcastic guy.

"You told us to get behind the columns," Yancy stammered. "I was just following orders."

"If one of your friends is hurt, you help them," Dad said. "I didn't see you try to help Stevie when the guardian swallowed him. I didn't see you try to help anyone . . . except yourself."

Yancy took a long swallow.

Dad sighed and reached into his toolkit. "Everyone, have a glass of milk. We all need it."

He handed us each a tall glass of milk, and I couldn't think of a time when milk had looked more delicious. I drank it down with deep gulps and felt all my pains and aches magically go away. When I'd finished the milk, I felt like a new person.

"I wish milk worked like this on Earth," Destiny mused. "It's all we'd ever need to get better!"

"Milk's great," Alex agreed. "Wow, I can't believe the fish can blast us this much, even with our armor on." We all nodded in grim agreement to *that*.

I looked at Dad, glad to see he had regained his strength and looked like himself again.

Alex was already smashing through blocks in the room. "I'm seeing if the crystal shard is here," she explained.

"I doubt it's close to the entrance, but it doesn't hurt," Dad said. "It also gives us a moment to catch our breath."

Alex approached a sea lantern on the wall and smashed it. There wasn't anything in it or under it. "Hmm," she said.

Meanwhile, Maison stepped up next to me. "What *was* it like, being inside the guardian?" she whispered in my ear. "My heart about stopped beating!"

"It was like being in a small, red room," I said. "It didn't hurt, but . . ." I shuddered. "I don't want to ever do it again."

Maison nodded sympathetically.

"All right, kids," Dad said, when he saw Alex had thoroughly searched the room. "It's time to get back out there."

From above, something in the ocean monument let out a roar.

CHAPTER 8

"WHAT WAS THAT?" I GASPED.

I heard another echoing roar, nearly as loud as the first one. It seemed to shake the walls and columns.

"It's probably the sound of the elder guardians," Dad said. "Remember, we're avoiding those."

I bit my lip. If they roared like that, I definitely didn't want to end up face-to-face with one!

We stepped out of our room and back into the watery hall, with Dad leading and Alex right behind him. I noticed Yancy stepped out last of all and had his head down as if he didn't want to look at anyone. Fine with me. After how he'd been acting today, I didn't mind not interacting with him!

"'Find the glow,'" Alex murmured to herself, mulling over Steve Alexander's words. "There's another sea lantern!" She hurried over to check it out. Soon her expression clouded because it was nothing.

"You kids all look for the crystal shard," Dad said. "I'll keep my eyes peeled for any guardians."

"There's one now!" Maison said.

A guardian had turned a corner and was coming at us. Yancy cringed and ducked behind a column as Dad swam over and battled the fish. I kept my eyes on Dad, making sure he was okay, despite the fact I knew I should have been concentrating on looking for the crystal shard. It was still only one guardian, and it didn't take Dad long to take care of it. I breathed a deep sigh of relief, making extra bubbles run out of my mouth and float toward the surface.

Then I put my head down and started searching. All I saw were lots and lots of prismarine blocks and a few sea lanterns. Alex went right to the sea lanterns, getting excited whenever she spotted a new one. Then she would look disappointed as each sea lantern turned up nothing. Meanwhile, Dad kept any stray guardians at bay.

"Pssst, Stevie," came a small, gargled voice.

It was Yancy, still behind a column. I ignored him.

"Pssssst, Stevie!" It was a little louder this time.

"What, Yancy?" I asked, frustrated.

"I want to talk to you."

"Then talk," I said. I had a feeling he wanted me to go over to him to hear whatever he had to say, like he was some baby who needed comforting. He was the oldest of all of us, not counting Dad. I couldn't believe what a chicken Yancy was being today.

Then again, maybe it wasn't all that surprising. Before Yancy was my friend, he was a cyberbully known by the name TheVampireDragon555. Back then he used to terrorize people online, all from behind the safety of his computer screen. Whether behind a screen or a column, Yancy could talk big and scary while keeping *himself* protected.

I knew that wasn't totally fair. After Yancy put his cyberbullying days behind him, he had risked his life for the Overworld and shown real bravery more than once. So what was his problem now?

"Can't you come here?" Yancy whispered.

"No, I'm looking for the crystal shard," I said. I swam farther away from Yancy, partly to cover more space, partly to get away from him. I thought I heard Yancy sigh, but it was cut off by another monument-shaking roar.

"Hey, I found something neat!" Maison called.

Glad for the distraction, I quickly made my way to Maison. She'd grabbed two columns and pulled herself into a little space to the side. As we all crowded around, we found a room chock-full of boxed gold that hung from the ceiling.

No, wait, it wasn't gold we were seeing. It was *sponges*. I had known that you could find them in ocean monuments. What I hadn't realized was that you could find so many. If Dad and I harvested these, we could fill up our whole supply shed!

"Should we take these with us?" Maison asked. "Would they be helpful?"

Dad shook his head. "They're already full of water, so they can't pull the water out of a room like we did earlier. You need a dry sponge for that. Just look through them to see if the shard is in here."

Maison and I swam through the sponges, poking around for anything glowing. Nothing. However, it did give Maison and me some time together.

"Do you know what's wrong with Yancy?" I asked.

"Lots of things are wrong with Yancy," she said jokingly.

"He's acting extra weird," I said, shaking my head. "I think he's slowing us down on this mission. He's barely moving."

"Just ignore him unless he's in trouble," Maison said. "We need to put our energies toward finding the shard."

She sounded so logical, and yet I still couldn't drop my feelings. We searched through all the sponges on the ceiling. But just as I turned, I found myself face-to-face with the eye of another guardian.

CHAPTER 9

THE GUARDIAN WAS SO CLOSE ITS EYE TOOK UP ALmost all of my vision. I immediately struck out at it with my sword, then yelped. The guardian's spikes were all out, and now I realized how much it hurt to hit them. It was like a special laser that just went through my sword arm. I had to quickly hit the guardian two more times, and both times I felt the sting. Then the guardian was gone.

It was my own fault. I was thinking too much about Yancy and the shard and not spending enough time watching where I was going and what was around me. Maison peeked out from behind a large sponge, her black hair floating all around her face.

"Are you okay, Stevie?" she asked.

"Yeah," I said, massaging my arm. "There's nothing in this room. Let's get back to the others."

I was still rubbing my arm when we joined up with them. Dad saw what I was doing and said, "Make sure you hit them when their spikes are down."

"Yeah . . ." I said, embarrassed. "I figured that one out."

"Ooh!" Alex cried out excitedly from ahead. "I found it!"

We all rushed to her, thinking she'd found the crystal shard. Even Yancy got out from behind his column and hurried over. But when we caught up to Alex, all I saw was an enormous, column-like structure in the middle of the monument, made out of dark prismarine. Alex started pounding it, knocking the dark prismarine away. Underneath she found blocks of real gold, not sponges.

"We can take some of this gold back, right, Uncle Steve?" Alex said, ready to start putting some in her toolkit.

"No," Dad said. "We only want the crystal."

I still saw Alex sneak a block of gold into her toolkit before she swam on. I decided there wasn't any point in telling on her.

"So we found sponges, and we found gold," I said. "But we're still not any closer to the crystal shard."

Another roar shook the monument and we all drew closer together.

Dad frowned. "If we go too far down either of these wings, we might run into the elder guardians. Let's keep going forward."

As we swam, I noticed the part of the ocean monument we were in was getting darker. I thought about Earth's deep ocean, where it was so pitch-black the fish needed to glow just to be able to see. Was the ocean monument going to keep getting darker and darker?

I opened my mouth to say something and I found it was hard to speak. My hand rushed to my throat. It wasn't actually getting darker! Our potions were running out!

Everyone else seemed to be noticing this at the same time as me. Dad said something to us, and I could only make out some of the words. It sounded like, "Get—potion—drink—"

We all knew what he meant. Everyone's hands dove into their toolkits (or, for Yancy, his backpack) and yanked out their potions.

As soon as I got down the Potion of Night Vision, everything got less dark and cloudy. I realized it was starting to get a little uncomfortable to breathe, though it wasn't too bad yet. And when I chugged down the Potion of Water Breathing, all that discomfort went away. Phew. There was definitely no way we could be down here without those potions.

That got me thinking.

We hadn't even explored a fraction of the ocean monument, but we'd already used up half our potions. And when the potions we'd just drunk lost their effect, that would be it. We'd be done.

CHAPTER 10

*T*HE SEA LANTERNS ARE TOO OBVIOUS, I THOUGHT while I saw Alex smashing at them and coming away disappointed. So was the gold. So where would Steve Alexander have wanted to stash away the crystal shard? Was it someplace with meaning, like with the crystal shard in the jungle temple? Or did he just sneak it behind one of these prismarine blocks so that we'd have to tear the whole place apart looking for it?

Minutes were passing, feeling fast and slow at the same time. Slow because we weren't finding anything useful. Fast because we knew the clock was running out on our air supply.

"There's another room with sponges," Dad said. "Stevie, check it out, and don't hit any guardians with their spikes out."

"Okay," I said, swimming that way. I tried not to feel embarrassed that he felt a need to remind me.

"Pssst, hey, hey, Stevie," whispered a gargled voice. Darn it. It was Yancy again.

I turned, and at least this time he was floating out in the open instead of hiding.

"Spill the beans, Yancy," I said. It was an Earth expression I'd learned from him. It didn't involve any actual beans.

It looked like Yancy really wanted to say something to me and just wasn't sure how.

"I'm sorry I haven't been the best today," Yancy finally said. He followed me into the space with all the sponges. It kind of felt closed off, with just the two of us there, and we were both looking among the sponges for the crystal shard or any clues.

I didn't say anything. I just kept looking. And I kept my eyes out for guardians.

"The truth is, I'm terrified down here," Yancy said.

"We all are," I replied matter-of-factly. Dad told me it was normal to get scared, but it wasn't normal to run from what you were scared of, unless there were no other options. And we had to find that crystal, so there *weren't* other options.

"No, it's different," Yancy said. "You see . . . I almost drowned when I was little."

This caught my attention. I hadn't known that.

Then again, there were lots of things I didn't know about Yancy.

"I was at the public pool with my parents," Yancy said. It sounded like he wanted to go into something deep.

"What's a public pool?" I asked, confused.

"A pool's like a lake with chlorine in it that you can swim in," Yancy said. "Public means anyone in the community could go there."

I didn't know what *chlorine* was, though I decided it didn't matter right then. Yancy went on, "I was probably about four. My parents told me to stay in the shallow end of the pool, because I didn't know how to swim yet. My mom was sunbathing and reading a book and my dad was resting with his eyes shut. There were other kids in the pool with me, but the bigger kids who could swim all went out to the deep end, where the water was about eight feet deep."

"Okay," I said. I wasn't sure where he was going with this.

"The bigger kids started making fun of me," he said. "There were other four-year-olds who could swim, so they said I was a baby. I wanted to show off, and swimming didn't look too hard. I went into the deeper water and tried to copy what they were doing."

The bigger kids didn't sound very nice to me. "And what happened?" I asked.

"I couldn't swim, and I went under," he said. "When I couldn't breathe, I started to panic. I couldn't have been under for too long, but every second felt like it was the end and I was never going to get out of the water. Panicking made it worse. Then the lifeguard—the person working there who makes sure nothing bad happens—dove in and pulled me out. He got me back on the pavement and I was choking and still scared. My dad showed up, and I was hoping he'd make me feel better. Instead, he was mad at me for not listening."

A dad who wasn't happy with something you'd done that was foolish? I could relate.

"And the kids were still making fun of me," Yancy said. "After that, I was just scared of swimming. I loved looking up stuff about the ocean, but I felt like a coward because I couldn't actually go swim in the ocean."

"Your ocean sounds too dangerous to swim in," I said.

Yancy shook his head. "I shouldn't have scared you about the Earth ocean. You don't need to be scared of it, you just need to *respect* it. Does that make sense? For years I didn't learn how to swim, and then Destiny finally taught me how to swim when I was twelve."

He said this as if it were supposed to be extremely embarrassing. I didn't know what age kids tended to learn to swim on Earth, so it meant nothing to me. But when I thought about it, I realized Maison was eleven and Destiny was twelve, and they both already knew how to swim. In fact, they looked more confident in their swimming than Yancy did.

"People learn how to do things at different ages," I said. It still didn't seem like a big deal to me.

"It's embarrassing to learn how to swim that late, and to be taught by your kid cousin," Yancy said.

I thought of my cousin, Alex. She was always doing impressive things, especially if it involved bows and arrows. Maybe the difference was we were the same age. If Alex were several years younger and that much better than me, I probably would have been embarrassed.

"You know how to swim now," I said. "Isn't that what matters? And you swam when we defeated the Endermen in the tunnel." That had been after we found the first Ender crystal shard.

"Yeah," Yancy said. "Water can still make me nervous, though. Especially this deep. Especially in this ocean. There wasn't that much water when we fought the Endermen in the tunnel, compared to all *this*. I thought fighting the Endermen was proof that I'd finally gotten over my fear of deep water, but as soon as we got in the boat and lost sight of land, I realized I was as scared as ever. In the Earth ocean, unless you do something foolish or aren't paying attention, probably nothing is going to attack you. Here, you *know* things are going to attack you."

"So that's why you tried scaring me with those pictures?" I said. "And why you played that stupid rock-paper-scissors game? That's cheating, you know." I made sure to peer over a sponge and look Yancy in the eyes when I said that.

Yancy dropped his eyes. "Yeah, I know," he said. "And I shouldn't have done it."

"And you want to go into a cage with a shark circling you?" I asked skeptically. If Yancy were as scared about water as he said he was, I didn't understand why he'd want to get in a shark cage!

"Well . . . yeah," he said. "I love sharks. I feel like people choose to be scared of them because of how they look instead of learning anything about them. Back when I was bullying people online, I kind of felt like a shark. No one wanted anything to do with me and they judged me without knowing me. So if they thought I was some jerk, I decided I was going to be some jerk. I don't want to be like that anymore. But no one changes overnight."

"What do you mean?" I asked.

"I mean I don't attack people like I used to, but I still hide from my fears," he said. "The way I used to hide behind the computer screen."

He let out a long sigh that sounded like a confession, as if he were thinking about all the things he'd done that he regretted now.

I felt some of my anger toward Yancy melting away. Things made more sense when I heard his story, and he was owning up to his mistakes now. I'd had a bad experience in the tunnel with the Endermen and all the flooding water, but that was more because I was exhausted and hurt by the time the water had flooded around me. I'd never had the sensation of not knowing how to swim and feeling I was going to drown and there was nothing I could do about it. I couldn't imagine how bad that must feel.

"It'll be okay, Yancy," I said. "You're showing a lot of bravery just being down here. I bet you'll be brave enough to go into a cage next to sharks someday."

He gave me a smile that said "thank you" better than words could. It was a nice moment.

A second later the moment was broken. An evil voice crowded into my head, and I realized I wasn't alone.

CHAPTER 11

*F*RIENDSHIP WILL ONLY WEAKEN YOU, STEVIE, SAID the menacing voice. It was so close it felt as if it could have been whispered in my ear. But I knew better. It was the voice of the Ender Dragon, speaking straight into my mind.

"Get out!" I shouted, gripping the sides of my head.

"Stevie, what is it?" Yancy cried, his eyes widening. "Is it . . . her?"

I knew she would never leave me alone for long. The Ender Dragon loved to torment me, to try to make me her servant. She whispered all sorts of sweet promises I knew were lies, but sometimes she sounded so convincing I believed her for a while. I needed to fight her evil power!

You think you can trust this boy, Yancy? she continued. *I tried to have a friendship once upon a time. There was one whom I would have given my life to protect, only to be betrayed by him.*

What was she talking about?

She chuckled cruelly. *Oh, Stevie, you think you know so much, yet you know so little. I will be free soon, even if you get this next crystal.*

It sounded like she was admitting that her minions couldn't get to the bottom of the sea. At the same time, I didn't doubt that her powers were growing stronger.

Of course, she went on, *you could get the crystal for me. For* us. *You and I could work together.*

That was definitely a lie. She only wanted the crystal for herself, no matter how much she attempted to make it appear otherwise.

Yancy was trying to speak to me in a frantic voice. I couldn't make out the words and I jerked as if I could shake the Ender Dragon out of my head. Then Yancy seemed to be calling to the others, telling them to get over here.

It's a very big monument, she said. *I could help you.*

The others were swimming over, alerted by Yancy. The Ender Dragon's voice sounded so loud in my head that I still couldn't make out their words when they tried talking to me. I could just see their scared faces. Right now, the only sound I could hear other than the Ender Dragon was the elder guardians' roars from above.

Even as we speak, you're losing air, she said. *Yancy knows what it feels like to almost drown. You'll know the same feeling soon enough, but there will be no "almost" about it.*

I couldn't stop shaking my head, trying to get her out. She was targeting my worst fears.

Accept it! she was yelling now. *You've lost!*

"You said friendships will only weaken you!" I shouted back. In front of me, the others heard and looked really confused. Since they couldn't hear the Ender Dragon's side of the conversation, it had to look especially confusing and chilling. "So why do you want to be friends with me?"

Friends? she repeated. *We are not talking about friendship. We are talking power, the power you and I could have together.*

I didn't know what to do. Dad grabbed hold of my shoulders, as if to brace me. I saw his mouth move and I helplessly, painfully shook my head at him.

Another voice.

Stevie, it called. It was a calm, strong voice. I'd heard it once before, but never again after that.

"Steve Alexander?" I whispered. Was it really him? Just the sound of that voice in my mind seemed to push the Ender Dragon back.

You must face your fears, he said.

No! the Ender Dragon hissed, furious. *Stevie, don't listen to him!*

Look inside yourself, Stevie, the other voice said. *Go deeper.*

Despite everything that was going on, Steve Alexander's voice had a calming effect on me. My eyes slowly drifted shut. I could hear my heartbeat and feel the ocean move around me. The ocean stopped being scary or magical. It just was. I felt its water and its animals. In my mind I could almost see the pufferfish and clownfish swimming a little outside of the monument. I felt the squids nearby, pushing forward with their tentacles.

Good, the strong voice said. *What did I say in my book?*

I thought back on the words written in Steve Alexander's book: *There is much yet to be discovered in the depths of the ocean. The guardians' lasers will burn you, so bring armor. To your left and to your right, there will be elder guardians. Avoid them as best you can. Find the glow, and find your treasure.*

What did all that mean?

I zeroed in on the last part.

To your left and to your right, there will be elder guardians. Avoid them as best you can. Find the glow, and find your treasure.

My eyes were still closed, and it was as if I could sense more of the ocean monument. It was as clear as reading a map. I saw where the elder guardian was in the left wing of the monument, and I saw where the elder guardian was in the right wing of the monument. They were even bigger than I had imagined: giant gray fish with their own share of spikes and their own single, staring eye in the middle of their foreheads. I did not want to mess with creatures that looked like that.

So then . . .

In my mind, I saw a purple glow.

And I knew where the crystal was hidden.

Go for it, Stevie, and don't doubt yourself, the kind voice said.

I opened my eyes and began swimming as quickly as I could. Everyone looked at me in shock. When they said my name, I could hear them again, but I ignored them, even when Dad called for me to come back. My whole being was concentrated on the crystal.

Good, good, the calm voice said. I could hear the Ender Dragon hissing her fury, yet her voice was being pushed back and the man's voice was moving forward so it was all I could hear in my mind. *Don't look back, Stevie. Go for the crystal.*

Yes, I thought. *Yes, I will. I* am.

For some reason I didn't feel terrified, even though I knew I had to go to the most dangerous place in the ocean's depths. I had to go into the lair of the elder guardian at the very top of the monument. The home of the elder guardian that made roars that shook the whole monument.

That was the only way the crystal could ever be ours.

CHAPTER 12

I LEFT THE SPONGE ROOM AND ENTERED THE FULLER, middle part of the ocean monument. Then I began to swim upward.

"Stevie!" Dad hollered. "Stop!"

"I know where the crystal is!" I shouted back without pausing. "Steve Alexander told me!"

"Did he just say what I thought he said?" Yancy asked, astonished.

I glanced over my shoulder and saw they were all following me now. Dad was swimming the quickest, and even though I could see Yancy was really trying now, he was still last in line.

"Are you sure about this?" Dad called. "It's not the Ender Dragon trying to trick you? You're going straight for the topmost elder guardian!"

"We don't want the elder guardians on the right or left!" I said. "We want the main one!"

"Stevie, slow down so we can catch up!" Dad said. "You can't go after that thing alone! You have no idea how strong it is!"

"There isn't time!" I said. "We're going to run out of air!"

I still had a slight sense of where things were, but now that I was moving with my eyes open and the voices had stopped, I didn't have the clear-as-a-map picture of the ocean monument in my head anymore. However, I had a good enough idea, and I was full of energy, ready to get this mission done.

What I didn't expect was for the whole figure of the elder guardian to flash before me then, causing a shudder to go through my entire body.

I cried out and swung at it with my sword. But the guardian I had seen was already gone and my sword sliced through nothing but water. What had happened?

"Did you just see that?" Destiny cried, shuddering.

"I know what that was!" Maison said. "In *Minecraft*, you see the elder guardian flash over your screen when it gives you Mining Fatigue."

"That means we're getting close," Dad said.

Seeing the elder guardian was like being splashed abruptly with freezing water. I was cold, startled, and shaken. When Steve Alexander had been talking to me, I had felt ready to take on the elder guardian. But now

I didn't feel so certain. If the elder guardian could do this to people without actually being near them, what would it be like to fight it face-to-face?

Then I remembered what Steve Alexander had said. That I had to face my fears. That I shouldn't doubt myself. Whether or not I could still feel him or hear his voice, I had to believe he was with me. And that he believed in me.

So I took a deep breath and kept swimming, with the others behind me.

The image flashed in front of me again and I felt the same ice-cold sensation pour over my body. I also thought I saw something purple and glowing.

Find the glow, and find your treasure.

There was a room in the ceiling above me, and I could see a small, square hole that led into it. I grabbed the edges of the hole and pulled myself through.

As soon as my head popped up, I saw it. An enormous elder guardian, even larger than I had sensed the other two elder guardians were. It took up almost the whole room, and was much more terrifying than any image Yancy had shown me in his book. First I saw its single, pinkish eye, which was partially covered by an angry-looking eyebrow that slanted down. Next I saw rows of jagged, blue-purple spikes pointing out of its body like spears. Each one of those spikes was bigger than my diamond sword.

A purple glow was rising from its midsection.

That had to be where the missing Ender crystal shard was. Inside the belly of the beast.

Telling myself not to be scared, I swam forward and struck out with my sword.

Argh, what was I thinking? Not doubting myself wasn't the same as charging forward without knowing what I was doing. Its spikes were out, and I felt the sting of pain zap through me. It hurt so much worse than hitting a regular guardian.

The others were pulling themselves through the hole and into the room with me.

"Holy cow," Yancy said.

"I've never seen an elder guardian that big!" Dad cried. "Back up, Stevie! Its spikes are out!"

If I backed up, I was sure it would get ready to shoot lasers at us, just like the regular guardians. If just hitting its spikes hurt worse than hitting a guardian, its lasers probably did more damage than anything we'd felt so far.

I didn't know how all of us could take this beast on. Our five weapons were nothing compared to a mob this size. And the Ender crystal was actually *inside* the monster, as if it had swallowed the shard!

An idea crossed my mind.

Oh, no, I thought. *Not that! Anything but that!*

Except I couldn't come up with any other ideas. I thought back to earlier in the boat, when Yancy and Destiny were arguing over whether sharks went around eating people. Sharks might not, but guardians did.

I'd been sucked inside a guardian once before and gotten out in one piece.

"Everyone, I'm going in!" I shouted. "Attack it from the outside and I'll attack it from the inside."

"Stevie, no!" Dad exclaimed. "That's too risky!"

I knew it was risky. I also knew I had the strangest feeling then, as if Steve Alexander were standing by my side, even though I couldn't see him. I couldn't even hear his voice anymore. It didn't matter. I knew what I had to do.

Instead of attacking the elder guardian, I flung myself straight for its face. Its enormous mouth gaped open like a nightmare, and the beast swallowed me whole.

CHAPTER 13

I WAS SURROUNDED BY THE RED WALLS OF THE ELDER guardian's insides. Like before, it was comparable to being in a red room, but so many times bigger.

And something was glowing right in front of me. Glowing like the fish in the bottom of the Earth's ocean, shining light to find their prey. I swam forward and my hand closed around the Ender crystal shard.

As soon as I did that, I could sense the elder guardian's power weakening a little. This crystal could be used as a weapon or as a power, and I realized the fish had held this crystal in its stomach for so many years that the magic had made it grow and grow. Now that I had my hand on its power, it might be more like fighting a normal elder guardian.

That still wasn't very reassuring, because normal elder guardians were still the most feared creatures in the sea. The elder guardian began to shake violently, as if it wanted to knock me out of its insides—or, as if it was attacking the others. My whole body got flung against the far red wall of its insides. I groaned at the impact.

Before I could recover, the fish jerked again. I stumbled across to the other side of it, hitting the red wall. I slashed with my sword. The wall glowed red for a second, which meant I'd made a good strike. The elder guardian jerked once more and I was hurled across the room.

Regaining my balance, I struck the wall again and again. Three hits was usually enough to take out most mobs. But the wall of the fish's insides only glowed red for a second and then nothing happened.

I started to feel panic rise up in my throat. Dad was right—this had been too risky of a plan. I'd actually fed myself to this monster!

"Steve Alexander!" I shouted. "What do I do now?"

Silence.

Steve Alexander had told me not to doubt myself, but he had disappeared when I needed him most. Why? Why would he do that to me?

Another voice answered me instead of Steve Alexander. *My, what a situation you have yourself in,* teased the Ender Dragon, enjoying this way too much. *Little Stevie listened to Steve Alexander and wanted to look heroic so badly that he doomed himself and his friends. Oh, how they are suffering trying to free you.*

I slashed out with my sword again, as if I could hit the elder guardian and the Ender Dragon at the same time. The elder guardian glowed red from the hit but still didn't vanish.

Your father was hurt earlier, the Ender Dragon gloated. *He's hurt again now, and he's your group's best warrior. What will happen when he falls? You're stuck in here; you can't help. Alex's arrows alone will be no match for the beast, and your poor Earth friends are not trained for ocean fighting.*

"It can't take that many hits to defeat this elder guardian!" I shouted. "You're wrong!"

Steve Alexander! I was thinking. *Come back! Why did you leave?*

The elder guardian will defeat the others, the Ender Dragon said. *At least their ends will be quick. But you'll be trapped inside there, left to wait until your potions stop working and you can no longer breathe.*

For a second my throat closed up, as if what she was predicting was already coming to pass. Then I shook my head and forced those fears away, shouting, "No!" I hit the elder guardian again with my sword. It was still thrashing around, knocking me to different places in its belly.

Or, the Ender Dragon said casually, as if we were just having a nice chat, *I could save you all. I could give you, your father, your cousin, and your friends the ability to continue breathing. I could get you out of that elder guardian and out of the ocean monument. You would only have to do one thing for me.*

She paused for the smallest second, letting the intensity build. I already felt myself getting chills, knowing the terrible deal she would offer.

Give me the crystal, she said, *and you will live.*

CHAPTER 14

FOR A MOMENT, THAT SOUNDED LIKE THE SMART-est thing to do. Give her the crystal and save all of us? Or stay here and be defeated?

But no. "*Never!*" I roared, and hit the elder guardian with all my might. There was an explosion of red light and the belly of the beast fell apart around me. The next thing I knew, I'd fallen back into the water, sputtering and trying to catch my breath.

"Stevie!" Dad said, grabbing me by my shoulders and hauling me up. I looked around. Everyone was there and still safe, though they looked a little worse for wear.

"You're okay!" I said.

"The crystal!" Alex marveled, her eyes glowing purple in the reflection. "The glow—Stevie, you were right! You were crazy to get eaten, but you were right!"

"I kept hitting the elder guardian, and nothing would happen," I said. "I thought nothing would stop it."

"It was a lot of work," Maison acknowledged. Then she grinned. "That doesn't mean we couldn't take care of it."

"Enough talk," Dad said. "We have what we need. Let's get back to the surface."

Count me in! I quickly slipped the Ender crystal shard into my toolkit to keep it safe. As much as I wanted to read the next part of the book right away to see what our next crystal adventure would be, I knew we had to wait until we'd reached shore and were safer—and able to breathe!

The crystal fell into the bottom of my toolkit, making everything inside the kit glow purple and look enchanted. I let a feeling of peace come over me. Maybe Steve Alexander couldn't always talk to me. Maybe he'd left me alone at that moment to let me know I could take care of the elder guardian without him. It had been a hard lesson, but I did feel stronger from it. And so glad I hadn't given in to the Ender Dragon, even when I was the most scared I could be.

Dad was still holding my shoulder and began pulling me with him as he swam. It was as if he thought I'd be extra fragile right then because of what I'd been through.

As we moved forward, I heard another roar. The walls and columns shook around us.

I felt another cold sensation sweep over me. For a second, my vision was filled with two giant eyes, from two different beings. It was two remaining elder guardians.

Just like that, they were gone.

"Mining Fatigue again," Maison said, shivering.

"That can't be right," Yancy objected hotly. "We're not anywhere near the other elder guardians. They're in two different parts of the monument."

In the back of my head, I heard a terrible laughter.

"Oh no," I said, realizing this mission wasn't anywhere near done. Elder guardians only flashed like that and gave Mining Fatigue if they were close. So if we weren't by the wings that had the other two elder guardians, that could only mean one thing.

A second passed. Another. And then two large elder guardians burst into the room, their lasers starting to spit purple as they prepared to attack.

CHAPTER 15

"DODGE!" DAD SHOUTED AS THEIR LIGHTS TURNED yellow and they shot lasers at us. We all lunged out of the way. I felt the heat of one of the lasers as it zipped right past me, lighting up my iron armor in a bright silver color.

Dad reached into his toolkit and pulled out his last sponge. In an instant, it sucked up most of the water in the room.

It was a great move! Now the two large fish were flopping in ankle-deep water. They still had their lasers and were still powerful, but they couldn't move as fast as they could before. And without all that water around, we could move *more* quickly!

"Attack them, kids!" Dad said. "Avoid their lasers!"

We dove at the elder guardians, attacking them from the sides. The two fish continued to fight and zap, but even though they were really big, they were nothing compared to that last elder guardian. Their yellow lasers shot at the walls, turning the room gold whenever they powered up.

Alex was going all out with her arrows, now that she could use them more easily. "Oh, this feels much better!" she said, yanking back her bowstring and sending arrows flying.

"How many hits did it take for you guys to get the last one?" I called out above all the laser and fighting noises.

"Too many," Dad said gruffly. "But these elder guardians are much smaller, and I was so worried about you then that I didn't think of using the sponge before!"

One of the elder guardians had managed to flop itself on its side and turn so that it was facing me now. It began to power up purple lasers, getting ready to nail me. I jumped out of the way. The laser hit the wall behind where I'd been standing, making it crumble a little.

Even as all this was going on, I was noticing regular guardians coming into the area. They were floating just outside the room where the sponge had no effect and there was still plenty of water. And they were turning purple so they could shoot at us. As I struck an elder guardian with my sword, I felt myself start to get blasted from behind.

I spun and went after the green-and-yellow guardian that had gotten me first. When I jumped right in front of it, it pulled back and its spikes dropped. That gave me a chance to hit it.

"Look out, Stevie!" Maison said.

I ducked. A yellow laser beam hit where my head had been. It was one of the elder guardians again, flipping onto its side.

I saw Alex line her bow with arrows and send them at the elder guardian that was closer to her. It did the trick, and the elder guardian vanished. That left the other one and all the regular guardians that kept sneaking up and shooting us from the edges.

"Concentrate on finishing off the last elder guardian!" Dad told us. "It's the strongest mob!"

I felt a regular guardian shock me from behind and gritted my teeth. If we took out the big one, that would let us all go after the small ones more easily. I hit the elder guardian above its one angry eye as the others all landed blows on it, striking it as it gleamed purple, preparing to shock us again.

When we all hit it together, the elder guardian vanished.

Then I got zapped from behind again. I immediately turned to the guardian that had done it. I had a few seconds before it would start to charge again, and I knew I had to get to it before it got me.

When I threw myself forward and struck the

guardian several times, it disappeared and dropped a pufferfish. So far all the guardians we'd defeated had dropped little prismarine shards, and I knew it was rare that guardians dropped other fish. So I grabbed the pufferfish and looked around me to see what had to be done next. With air in the room and Dad and Alex able to move more freely, they quickly took out most of the floating guardians.

Then there were only two guardians left, and Maison went after one while Alex shot her arrows at the other. Both fish disappeared, dropping more prismarine shards.

"Phew, glad that's over," Yancy moaned. We were all panting and trying to catch our breaths while Dad passed healing milk out to us. As I drank, I felt renewed. We had our Ender crystal shard and we had defeated all three of the elder guardians! We could finally get out of this awful place!

Wait a second.

Was it just me, or did it seem a little darker?

I sucked in a choking breath. The very last of our potions were running out!

CHAPTER 16

"**D**AD!" I CRIED, PANICKED.

"I know," he said, putting his hands to his forehead. "I feel it too."

"We'll just hurry up to the boat," Alex said quickly.

"There isn't enough time," Dad replied. "Even if we leave now and don't run into any more hostile fish, the surface is too far above us."

I saw Yancy go skeleton-white. Alex huffed, "That can't be right! Uncle Steve, what should we do?"

"Here," I said, thrusting out my hand and holding the pufferfish I'd just gotten. "You still have Nether wart, and we have plenty of water here. Make another Potion of Water Breathing."

Dad grabbed the pufferfish. "It won't be enough for all of us."

But still, he began moving blocks around swiftly to make himself a makeshift brewing stand.

"Um, um, let me think," Yancy said anxiously. "In the game, there are ways to make little air pockets."

"We can make all the air pockets we want, but they won't get us all the way to the surface," Dad said, hastily making the potion.

"Hold on!" I said. "I know! I saw pufferfish not far from the monument. I could go get them!"

"It doesn't work that way," Dad said. "You can only get pufferfish by fishing. We'd have to go back to the boat and make a fishing rod, and that won't work."

"On Earth, sometimes people fish with nets," Yancy said. "Maybe we can make something like that."

With quick mixing, Dad had turned the pufferfish, Nether wart, and water into a bottle of pink potion. We all looked at it with hungry, desperate eyes.

"Hey, I know," Yancy said. "My backpack!"

"Your backpack?" Dad said doubtfully, not following.

"If someone goes with me, we can probably steer the pufferfish into my backpack and zip it up," Yancy explained.

"I've never heard of such a thing!" Dad frowned, as if he found this idea offensive. "You catch fish by fishing with a fishing rod!"

"I know *Minecraft* used to just be a game to me and it's a real world to you," Yancy said. "But one thing I learned by playing *Minecraft* is that there isn't just one way to do a lot of things. That's the same way in real life, whether it's Earth or here."

I looked at Dad. He was getting harder to see as the whole world gradually got darker. Thank goodness there was still air in this room, or we'd be dealing with that too!

"I think I know how we can do this," I said. "Yancy and I can split the potion so we'll be able to breathe a little longer, and we'll go out and get the pufferfish. I remember where I saw them, and Yancy can help with the backpack."

"I've never split a potion before," Dad said, mulling this over. "I believe it would still work, but you'd only be able to breathe for half the time the potion would normally last."

"We have to move quickly, before we can't see at all," I said. In the back of my mind, I wondered what I was getting us into. Judging by Yancy's paler-than-pale face, he was thinking the same thing.

"We'll come with you," Maison said.

"Yeah, you can't go alone," Alex said, ready to muscle in.

Right then a blast of yellow flew out from behind us and hit Alex in the arm. She cried out, more startled and angry than anything else. Alex turned her furious eyes at the latest guardian to sneak up on us. A few more guardians were behind it.

"Do it, Stevie," Dad said, eyeing our new attackers. "You and Yancy. If we all go, there won't be enough air, and I need to stay to keep the guardians at bay here. Leave your crystal with me for protection, but take your sword!"

He was shoving the new Potion of Water Breathing into my hand and going with Alex to take out the guardians that were piling on the attacks again. I set down my toolkit, knowing the crystal was still safely stored at the bottom of it.

I turned to Yancy. It was getting twilight-dark now, which meant I couldn't really make out the look on his face.

"I should have thought through this before I opened my mouth," he said, not sounding very pleased. "Going out there is the last thing I want to do!"

Was Yancy backing out on me?

Then I noticed his mouth quirked a little and I thought he might actually be smiling. "Well, let's face this head on," he said. "If this won't get me ready to go into a cage with sharks, nothing will."

Despite how nervous I was, I felt a smile spreading over my own face. I swigged half the drink and handed the rest to Yancy. The two of us sneaked to the edge of the room and peered out where the water was. I could make out little blobs of yellow, and of orange and black. I knew those colors were the schools of pufferfish and clownfish.

"Are you ready?" I asked Yancy, who was braced at the edge of the monument, ready to jump back into the water.

He hesitated.

"Do you want to rock-paper-scissors it?" Yancy asked.

"Yancy—" I began, frustrated.

"Because I'll let you win," he said cheerfully, if a little regretfully, and lunged out. That Yancy! As soon as I realized what he was doing, I leaped out too, going into the darkness of the deep ocean.

CHAPTER 17

RAN THROUGH THE WATER WHILE YANCY SWAM NEXT to me, kicking his legs and making big swoops with his long arms.

"There could still be guardians," I said. "Keep your eyes peeled."

"Yeah, because my sight is so good right now," he said sarcastically, bubbles rolling out of his mouth.

As things got darker, I understood why Dad thought the Potion of Night Vision was so important under the sea. Down here it still wasn't as dark as at the bottom of the Earth ocean, where you needed lights to see. But everything was getting murky and less detailed, so I couldn't make out particulars anymore. If I hadn't been able to see and identify the pufferfish earlier thanks to the Potion of Night Vision, I would have just thought those yellow blobs could have been anything. And who knew what other dangers could arise because of how hard it was to see our surroundings? We might not be able to see the guardians until they started to light up to shock us. Or we might not even see them before feeling the bite of their lasers!

"Have you ever gone fishing with a net on Earth?" I asked, hoping he had some experience in this.

"The real question is, have I ever gone fishing, ever?" Yancy said. "And the answer is: no."

That didn't sound very assuring.

"I'd never even been in a boat before today," Yancy went on. "You?"

"I've fished from boats," I said. "But not anything like this."

A moment of silence hung between us. I thought I'd like the sound of a silent ocean, free of mysterious roars, but this silence was creepy in its own way. It let all the bad thoughts rush in, bigger and more oppressive than any elder guardian.

"Yancy," I said. "If this doesn't work, do you have any other ideas? What would you do if you were playing *Minecraft* and this happened?" He might have a unique perspective that wouldn't cross Dad's mind, so I wanted to hear his thoughts.

"What would I do?" Yancy said in a depressed voice. "Shut down the game without saving and start over."

"Oh, no," I said. It turned out I *didn't* want to hear

his thoughts. Was it possible to feel seasick *under* the water?

"But that's cheating," Yancy said. "We're just going to have to make this work, if you know what I mean. And you were really brave earlier, going after that elder guardian and getting the Ender crystal shard. When I saw that, I thought: wow, if Stevie can do that, I can get over my fears too."

"But Steve Alexander told me to do that, so I knew it would work!" I insisted. "This is different!"

"Ah, because it's a patented Yancy-and-Stevie idea?" he said. "You know, when Steve Alexander tried new things, it sounds like he faced a lot of resistance too."

"Patented?" I repeated, baffled.

The yellow blobs were getting closer. Yancy sidled up next to them and opened his backpack wide. "Okay, Stevie, steer them in," he said.

I began swimming at the pufferfish. They turned away from me and swam around Yancy—not into the backpack. Darn it, this wasn't working!

"Try again," Yancy said, sounding like he was trying to be patient.

My stomach tensing, I tried again to push the fish into the backpack. The fish still weren't behaving the way I wanted them to. They kept turning away from Yancy at the same time that they were turning away from me.

"I can't get them to go the right direction!" I yelled, frustrated.

"Here," Yancy said. The next thing I knew, he'd shoved the backpack into my arms. "Hold it open for me."

I did, startled to see Yancy taking charge. I watched nervously as he went to the fish and started to steer them. When they tried to slip past me, he put his long arms out to stop them. Fenced in by his long arms, the fish moved into the backpack instead.

"Whoo, got it!" Yancy cheered.

I tried to zip the backpack up, but had trouble. We didn't exactly have zippers in the Overworld! "It's caught!" I said, afraid that the fish would all swim back out.

"Give me that," Yancy said, taking the backpack from me. He zipped it up. "There," he said. "Now we just have to get back."

We turned toward the ocean monument. Without better eyesight, it looked eerie now, not at all magical. I could vaguely see a purple glow, and figured that was the Ender crystal shard. I hoped the others were doing okay while fighting the guardians!

I opened my mouth to holler that we had the puffer-fish, just in case they could hear us. But before I could make a sound, a guardian came barreling at us, already lit up with yellow sparks.

CHAPTER 18

"YANCY!" I SAID, TRYING TO WARN HIM. IT WAS already too late. The guardian blasted me and Yancy grabbed my shoulders when I slumped over in pain.

"I'll take Earth fish over you annoying little mobs any day!" he said. Once I'd recovered a little, the two of us were after the guardian before it could recharge. Getting close to it made it back up, and I hit it over and over with my sword while Yancy beat at it with his backpack. I saw a brief red glow and knew we'd gotten that guardian. That was close!

I took a deep breath and felt myself choking on it. What was happening? I tried to take another deep breath and realized I couldn't. I could only take small, shallow breaths, and I could barely even do *that*.

I looked at Yancy, horror-struck. When I tried to

say something, I didn't hear my gargled voice. Instead I could only hear a weird choking sound. I'd lost my ability to talk! That meant the Potion of Water Breathing was almost used up!

Yancy was making the same sound, so he must have been trying to talk to me as well.

My head snapped forward to where I was seeing the purple glow. We weren't too far from the room Dad had drained of water, but we weren't exactly close, either. Our only hope was that the potion would last long enough to get us there!

We both started moving our arms and legs like crazy, as if this could make us go faster. No matter what we did, we could only swim slowly. I put my hand out as if I could grab the monument and pull it closer, or measure how far away it was. My hand slipped uselessly in the water, the monument still so far out of reach.

And then the potion just gave out and I couldn't breathe at all. Everything was dark, so dark. I wanted to claw at my throat. *So this is what it feels like,* I thought. *This was how Yancy felt when he was in the pool.* Except this time there was no lifeguard to save us, and no person with enough Potion of Water Breathing to swim out and help us.

I felt my lungs heat up like a torch and every inch of me wanted to take a breath. I had to fight that instinct because I knew I'd only suck in salty ocean water. The bursting feeling in my lungs kept getting worse. Even being in the belly of the elder guardian had been better than this, because I could still see in there. I could still *breathe*!

The purple glow was just ahead, and I could tell we must be close. I saw something move. I startled, thinking it was another guardian coming after us. We didn't need more attacks right now! But instead of another shocking blast, I felt a hand grab me. It was Dad's hand. The next thing I knew, I was being pulled back into the air-filled room of the ocean monument. Destiny was pulling Yancy in, and Maison and Alex were taking care of the guardians that were still attacking the room.

I sucked in a huge, gasping breath. Yancy unzipped his backpack and out fell our collection of pufferfish.

"You did it," Dad said, amazed and grateful. He snatched up the pufferfish and began working at his brewing stand.

"We won't be able to see much, but all we'll need to do is get back to the boat," Dad was saying as he whipped up six Potions of Water Breathing. I grabbed my toolkit, glad it was still safe and sound.

"Steve!" Maison called to Dad. "There are more guardians coming!"

"Here, drink your potions," Dad said, handing them all out. We chugged them down, and bubbles began coming out of our mouths, meaning that the potions were working.

"We did it, Stevie!" Yancy said, laughing as bubbles spilled out of his mouth. In spite of his laughter, there was still a lot of nervous energy about him. "I say we get to the surface and call this a day!"

CHAPTER 19

As we swam up and out of the ocean monument, the guardians followed us. It was harder to fight them in the middle of the dark ocean, where there was nothing to hide behind. As we swam, we were getting zapped by lasers every few seconds.

"Hold on, kids," Dad said. "We're almost there!"

I felt myself get blasted again. Ugh, I hated those fish so much! Another blast hit me but I tried to keep my eyes ahead. As we got nearer to the surface, it got lighter and easier to see. I could see the brown outline of our little boat rocking on top of the waves.

I burst out of the water, inhaling loudly. Sunlight! Clouds! A baby blue sky! I was thrilled to be in a world I could recognize again. The others were all appearing out of the water at the same time and together we scrambled to get into the boat.

Something was already waiting for us there.

It was the guardian that had lunged into the boat earlier and made Yancy and me jump overboard! I had completely forgotten about it, and here it was, still flopping away! Yancy's parrot, Blue, was flying overhead and whistling in an angry way, as though he didn't like having the guardian there.

"Another one!" Dad said with a snarl, hitting the fish. Stunned, I watched as Yancy jumped forward and also hit the fish, helping Dad. Just like that, the guardian was gone. Blue gratefully flew back to us and perched himself on Yancy's shoulder.

"Don't look down," Destiny said.

We all looked down. A set of guardians was circling the boat, just like Destiny said sharks did with their prey. The next second, they began to blast us.

"Not so fast, fishes," Alex said, pulling out her bow and arrows. She began hitting them, one by one, where they were swarming just beneath the surface. Meanwhile, Dad was steering the boat as quickly as he could toward shore. I joined Alex in fighting the guardians, reaching down with my diamond sword to strike them.

"They're following us!" I said. No matter how quickly Dad moved the boat, the guardians kept circling under it. And no matter how many we made disappear, more kept coming up to attack. At this point Dad was steering the boat and the rest of us were busy keeping the guardians back. And we were still being blasted regularly.

"We just need to get to land," Dad said. "They can't follow us far on shore, and we'll get milk from the village there!" As he said that, he got blasted by a yellow laser. Angry, I hit the fish that had shot Dad, glad that my diamond sword cut down on it and made it disappear.

A thin sliver of brown and green showed up on the horizon. Land!

I had never realized how magical land looked until this moment. I'd just taken it for granted. When Dad pulled us up onto the shore and we all vaulted out of the boat and onto the solid ground, it was like being home.

The guardians leaped onto the shore with us, only to flop there uselessly, making noise. They were no longer a threat. We could leave them behind. We could leave it *all* behind.

"That was remarkable," Dad said as we stumbled farther ashore, out of the guardians' reach. "Stevie and Yancy, your idea saved us all from drowning. Alex, Maison, and Destiny, you fought so well against the guardians. I know they're tough mobs to beat. And Stevie . . ."

He turned to me. "I never would have thought to look for the Ender crystal shard with the elder guardian in the top of the monument. That was all you. Maybe

Alexandra was right. Maybe having you all as a task force isn't the risky idea I thought it was."

I breathed in these compliments the way I breathed in sweet, fresh air. It made me smile. Dad was actually really impressed with all of us and what we'd done in the ocean monument!

"Hey, Stevie," said a voice from behind me.

This time I wasn't annoyed when Yancy slipped up to me, wanting to talk. Blue was still perched on his shoulder and looking very happy to have his person back.

"Yeah?" I asked, unsure what Yancy would say after all we'd been through.

"Thanks for listening to me, and helping me out back there," he said, grinning.

"I knew you had it in you," I said.

"Did you really?" he asked, looking touched.

"Well, I don't know," I said more honestly. Yancy's smile fell. So I quickly went on, "I think you were the bravest of us all because you were the most scared. Steve Alexander said I had to face my fears. You did all that and more."

I was used to people getting braver as they got older. It was a little strange to me to have a big, tough-looking kid like Yancy being scared and not wanting to admit it.

"I have a favor to ask you, Stevie," he went on, smiling again as we headed, dripping, to the nearby village for milk. Dad was already opening Steve Alexander's book to the last page we'd been able to read and pulling the Ender crystal shard out of my toolkit so we could read it. Soon we'd know where our next adventure would take us.

"What's that?" I asked, a little uncertain.

"When I go into the shark cage, will you go with me?"

A shark cage? After all that?

"All right," I finally said. "But only if you go first!"

READ ON FOR AN EXCITING SNEAK PEEK AT THE FIFTH BOOK IN

Danica Davidson's
Unofficial Overworld Heroes Adventure series

Available wherever books are sold in June 2018
from Sky Pony Press

CHAPTER 1

THE ENDER DRAGON WAS ABOUT TO ESCAPE FROM her prison. I could feel it all the way down to my bones, like a cold wind. The monsters in the land had been growing stronger for weeks, and the nights had gotten so long we barely saw the sun anymore.

Then there was her voice: it kept taunting me, inside my head, promising to do evil deeds if I didn't bow to her. The Overworld's only hope was to find the last crystal shard that my ancestor Steve Alexander had hidden. With it, we could create the ultimate weapon to defeat her.

But we had hit a dead end.

"Read it again," my cousin Alex demanded.

I sighed and read the newest passage we'd decoded in Steve Alexander's enchanted book. We'd already read it a dozen times. After each new crystal we found, the enchantment in the book let us read a little more of the text—but this clue was far too vague. So far Steve Alexander had also been giving us maps in the book to find the next crystal, but we'd gotten no map with this one. And time was running out!

"*For its safety, the final crystal shard has been taken from this world and given to Maya,*" I read. "*Seek out the earth woman.* Alex, that's all it says."

"This is just great," muttered Yancy sarcastically, raking his hand through his dark hair. "We have no map, and apparently this crystal is floating around somewhere on Earth. A tiny little planet which, according to the Internet, has a radius of a mere 3,959 miles. You know, just a quick stroll."

"It's almost like Steve Alexander doesn't want us to find the last crystal shard," murmured Destiny, nervously biting at her fingernails.

"I don't think that's it," Maison argued. She was my best friend, and the first person I had met from Earth. Right now we were all sitting in her bedroom, near her computer that acted as her portal to the Overworld. Or "*Minecraft,*" as people on Earth called it. "Whenever Steve Alexander gets vague about things, he usually wants us to dig deeper."

"Yeah, and I'm digging," Yancy said, clicking on his phone. Blue, the pet parrot he had tamed in the jungle biome, was perched on Yancy's shoulder, happily chirping. At least that bird was unaware of the stress the rest of us were feeling.

"If we can't track down the crystal, you'd think we'd at least be able to track down Maya, the Earth woman who helped Steve Alexander imprison the Ender Dragon in the first place," he went on. "But you know what the problem is with that? Well, there's the fact that she apparently lived thousands of years ago, before most human cultures had writing systems. Second, when I Googled the name 'Maya,' I got about a million hits. It showed up in all sorts of ancient cultures, not to mention modern ones, so we can't even narrow down where she might have lived. That's not even counting all the cultures that have disappeared over time, so we don't even have records of the names used."

I'd never thought of cultures disappearing. Was that like how we'd find old, forgotten temples in the Overworld and have no idea who'd made them? It hadn't occurred to me that Earth might have that, too.

"What does all that mean?" I asked.

"It means," Yancy said, "that Steve Alexander is no help on this one. We're down to the last crystal shard, and he's bailed on us. After all that talk about being a hero. What a loser."

Alex jumped up, furious. "Steve Alexander is the greatest hero the Overworld has ever seen, and he's our great-great-great-whatever grandfather! Don't you be talking about him like that!"

"Fine," Yancy said, tossing his cell phone into Alex's hands. "Then you find the crystal shard, and Maya."

Alex frowned. "I don't know how to use this contraption!"

Alex and I were from the Overworld, while Maison, Destiny, and Yancy all came from Earth. Alex and I knew how to make our own food and build our own homes and create our own weapons. Maison, Destiny, and Yancy knew how to use cell phones and computers and the Internet. We came from very different worlds, but we were still friends.

We were also all part of the Overworld Heroes task force, which had been created by my aunt, Mayor Alexandra. It was supposed to be our mission to stop the Ender Dragon from escaping from the End. She'd been threatening to do so for a while, and if she did, her first mission would be to take over the Overworld and go after Steve Alexander's descendants. That meant Alex, Aunt Alexandra, Dad, and me. She hated Steve Alexander for locking her in the End thousands of years ago. She'd been biding her time, waiting for revenge, ever since.

I ran the crystal over the book's pages. Normally using the newest crystal shard would light up more words so we could read. But all these pages were blank. And they stayed blank, crystal or no crystal.

"I think we'd probably have better luck using the original tools Steve Alexander gave us, instead of using the Internet," Maison said quietly. She had been acting really thoughtful while the rest of us were panicking. "They wouldn't have had the Internet back then, so he and Maya wouldn't have put clues there."

"See? This thing has no answers." Alex threw the phone back at Yancy, and he caught it as it struck him in the chest. "You people on Earth have all these things that are supposed to make your lives easier," Alex said, "but they don't answer the hard questions!"

"Hey, at least we live in a world that isn't overrun with monsters every night," Yancy shot back. Unlike Earth, darkness in the Overworld brought with it an onslaught of zombies; giant, red-eyed, spiders; armed skeletons; creepers; and other monsters we called "mobs." "Maybe if you had more technology, you would have figured out how to get rid of them by now."

Alex's face turned so red it looked like she was about to spit lava. When she opened her mouth to yell something at Yancy, I turned away and tried to clear my thoughts. I knew they were only fighting because they were stressed, but it wasn't going to do any good. Destiny looked miserable and hopeless, while Maison was staring out the window at the cold, rainy day, her mind clearly far away. I went to sit next to Maison.

While Yancy and Alex were arguing, I kept remembering what Yancy had said about Steve Alexander: *What a loser.*

Was he right? Everyone in the Overworld honored Steve Alexander's name, but when you looked at Steve Alexander's own writing, it often sounded like he didn't think he was so heroic. And the Ender Dragon kept hinting that the Steve Alexander we thought we knew wasn't the real Steve Alexander. Then again, she was always lying and manipulating and trying to destroy worlds. Steve Alexander wanted to *save* worlds.

Except now he'd left us stranded. It wasn't fair. Why would he even give us such a weak clue?

"What do you think?" I asked Maison.

"Maya can't be alive anymore, so it's not like we can seek her out," Maison said. "And that must be who he means by 'the Earth woman.'" She thought for another moment. "Unless . . ."

That "unless" was enough to get my heart pounding. Right then, *any* idea was enough to get my heart pounding.

My thoughts were interrupted by a screaming sound.